S0-BEF-210

Toopy and Binoo™

Books inspired by the television series

Bibliothèque et Archives nationales du Québec and
Library and Archives Canada cataloguing in publication

Jolin, Dominique, 1964-
[Grimace. English]
Binoo Blows Raspberries
(Toopy and Binoo)
Translation of: La grimace.
For children.

ISBN 978-1-55389-047-8

I. Tremblay, Carole, 1959- . II. Simon, Karen.
III. Title. IV. Title: Grimace. English.
V. Series: Jolin, Dominique, 1964- . Toopy and Binoo.
PS8569.O399G7413 2009 jC843'.54 C2009-940328-5
PS9569.O399G7413 2009

This text is adapted from an episode of the television series *Toopy and Binoo* produced by Spectra Animation Inc., with the participation of Treehouse.
Original script by Anne-Marie Perotta and Tean Schultz
Writing director: Katherine Sandford

We would like to thank Télé-Québec and
Treehouse for their collaboration.

© 2004 Spectra Animation Inc. All rights reserved.
From the collection Toopy and Binoo by Dominique Jolin published by
Dominique et compagnie, a division of Les éditions Héritage inc.
Toopy and Binoo is a trademark of Dominique et compagnie, a division
of Les éditions Héritage inc.

This text may not be republished, reprinted, adapted, modified or reproduced
by any means, whether electronic or mechanical, including by photocopy or microfilm,
without the prior written consent of the publisher.

© Les éditions Héritage inc. and Spectra Animation inc. 2009
All rights reserved.

Collection director: Carole Tremblay
Editor: Jacqueline Snider
Artistic and graphic direction and *Toopy and Binoo*
typeface design by Primeau Barey

Legal Deposit: 3rd Quarter 2009
Bibliothèque et Archives nationales du Québec
National Library of Canada

Dominique et compagnie
300 Arran Street, Saint-Lambert, Quebec, Canada J4R 1K5
Tel.: 514 875-0327 Fax: 450 672-5448
E-mail: dominiqueetcie@editionsheritage.com

www.dominiqueetcompagnie.com

Printed in China

We acknowledge the support of the Canada Council for the Arts for our publishing program.

We acknowledge the financial support of the Government of Canada through the
Book Publishing Industry Development Program (BPIDP) for our publishing activities.

Government of Québec–Publishing Program and Tax Credit Program–Gestion SODEC.

Binoo Blows Raspberries

Text by Dominique Jolin and Carole Tremblay
English Text by Karen Simon

From the original script by Anne-Marie Perotta and Tean Schultz
Illustrations taken from the television series *Toopy and Binoo*

Toopy is reading a book to Binoo.
He's on the last page.
"And so all the monsters stayed
best friends in the world for ever
and ever. THE END!"
"Oh, what a nice story,"
Toopy says.
But Binoo doesn't think so...
"What's wrong?" asks Toopy.
"Are you afraid of monsters?"
Binoo nods his head.
"Aha! I have just what you need,"
says Toopy.

Toopy takes another book.
"This is the perfect book for you, Binoo. It explains
what to do if you're scared."
He turns to the first page and reads.
"Are you afraid of Blue Monsters with six eyes and
funny little green horns?"
Yes he is! Binoo is afraid of Blue Monsters.
"Well then, if this kind of monster scares you," continues Toopy,
"all you have to do is go... Ppbblltt!!!"
Toopy sticks out his tongue and makes a terrrrrible face.

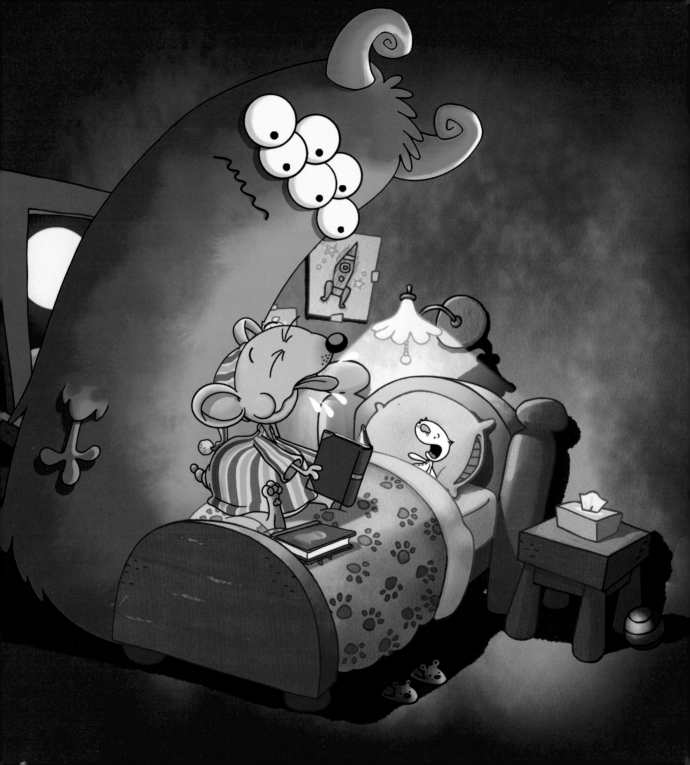

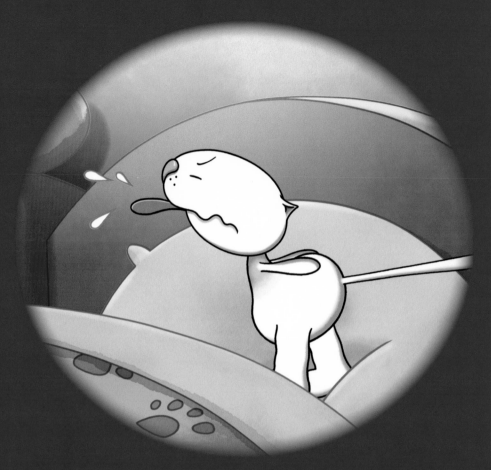

"It's really easy," says Toopy.
"Go ahead and try it, Binoo!"

Binoo sticks out his tongue and makes
a terrrrrible face. "Ppbbltt!!!"
Poof! The Blue Monster is gone, even before
Toopy had time to see him!
"You're fantastic, Binoo! I'm sure you can
make any monster disappear."

Toopy continues reading.
"Are you afraid of terrible Caterpillar Monsters
with four arms and lots of teeth?"
Toopy laughs.
"Caterpillar Monsters! That sounds funny!
I'd really like to see one!"
But Binoo *does* see one, and he doesn't
think it's funny at all.

"To get rid of Caterpillar Monsters," says Toopy, "you just have to go... Ppbbltt!!!"

Toopy sticks out his tongue. Now Binoo tries it. "Ppbbltt!!!" Poof! The Caterpillar Monsters are gone!

"That's fantastic, Binoo. You're learning fast,"
says Toopy, turning the page.

"Look, Ah-Choo Monsters! That's so silly!"
cries Toopy. "A monster that sneezes before he
catches you. I'm sure that's just made up,"
adds Toopy laughing.
Uh-oh! Toopy doesn't know that
there's one right behind him!

The Ah-Choo Monster starts walking toward
Binoo... he comes closer... and closer...
Toopy still doesn't see him. Toopy continues to read.
"If you're afraid of the Ah-Choo Monster,"
says Toopy, "just go Ppbblltt!!!"

Oh no! It looks like the Ah-Choo Monster is getting
ready to sneeze! Binoo sticks his tongue out
fast as far as it will go. "Ppbblltt!!!"
Poof! The Ah-Choo Monster is gone. Phew!

Toopy turns another page.
"This is a really good one,"
says Toopy. "Listen to this, Binoo!
Have you heard of the terrible
Feather-Fingered Tickle Monster?
I wouldn't want to meet one
of those!"

While Toopy is explaining how to
get rid of one, a Feather-Fingered
Tickle Monster appears and
begins to tickle Binoo.

Binoo sticks out his tongue, but he is
laughing so hard that his raspberry doesn't scare
away the monster. "Ppbblltt!!!..."
"I think you can do better than that, Binoo,"
says Toopy, without raising his eyes from the book.
Binoo tries again. "Ppbblltt!!!" And again.
"Ppbblltt!!!" The third try works! Poof!
The Feather-Fingered Tickle Monster is gone!

Toopy closes his book, laughing.
"That's it! Bravo, Binoo! So,
now you know what to do if
something scares you, right?"
Binoo smiles and sticks his
tongue out hard... "Ppbblltt!!!"

Poof! The monster book is gone!
Toopy and Binoo have a good laugh.